ALEXANDER LERNET-HOLENIA

MONA LISA

Translated from the German
by Ignat Avsey

PUSHKIN PRESS
LONDON

Pushkin Press
71–75 Shelton Street
London WC2H 9JQ

Mona Lisa first published in German in 1937 as *Mona Lisa*

© Alexander Dreihann-Holenia 2015

Illustrations © Neil Gower 2015

English language translation © The Estate of Ignat Avsey, 2015

First published by Pushkin Press in 2015

0 0 1

ISBN 978 1 782271 90 1

Set in Monotype Baskerville by Tetragon, London

Proudly printed and bound in Great Britain by TJ International,
Padstow, Cornwall on Munken Premium White 90gsm

www.pushkinpress.com

MONA LISA

the Love that moves the sun and the other stars

Dante, *The Divine Comedy*,
Paradiso, XXXIII, 145

TOWARDS THE END OF 1502, Louis XII, King of France, summoned one of his marshals, Louis de la Trémoille, and charged him to proceed immediately to Milan, where he was to raise an army and hurry to Naples to the relief of the two French governors, de Aubigny and the Duke of Namur, who had lately suffered serious losses at the hands of the Spaniards.

"And I trust, sir," the King went on, "you will be able to acquit yourself of this commission with your customary prowess. You shall not be left wanting anything. I send you forth not only with my own blessing, but also hereby give you leave as you make your way through Rome to seek the Holy Father's blessing. However, in case the Holy Father should refuse to anoint your arms, I give you full permission to urge His Holiness, with the help of those selfsame arms, to vouchsafe them his blessing. Furthermore, select as many of my noblemen as you deem fit to accompany you on your way. The flower of my nobility will be honoured and pleased to serve under you and personally to provide armour and equipment for you and your retainers. Also, you will have at your service a number of clerics whose upkeep and maintenance will devolve upon the Church. I shall take the sin of that upon myself. Additionally, I expect the good people of Amboise in Milan to cast the requisite number of ordnance, furnish the requisite number of ensigns, standards and trumpet banners, and supply a sufficient quantity of drums, kettledrums and trumpets. The cost of the undertaking is to be met from the municipal funds. You will of course have at your disposal as many horse and foot as you shall need, fed and nourished off the land, so help you God."

Here, while Louis appeared to ponder whether he should offer La Trémoille dominion over the sun, the waters, the air and the ground they stood on, for the upkeep of which God Himself was to be charged responsible, he bethought himself; and after staring for a while into the indeterminate middle distance past the Marshal with the vacant expression of one who at all costs refuses to talk of money, he added:

"As I said, you shall be wanting for nothing, my dear sir. You will be showered with glory, you will lead the army to victory and the splendour of our arms will spread far and wide. One more thing, though! I trust that you will also take the opportunity of recouping the cost of this campaign. Be sure therefore that you levy from the territories for whose sake we are making such sacrifices all necessary and fitting reparations, be it in the form of direct payments or precious objects, jewels, costly tapestries and suchlike things. For this is my express wish and command.* And so," concluded the King, "goodbye, and may God be with you!"

With these words he extended his hand to La Trémoille, placing it as though on a cushion on the plumed hat which the Marshal held out to him; and La Trémoille, after bowing and kissing the King's hand, took a step back. The King however mounted his horse and rode off on a stag hunt in the Forest of Senlis.

---

* *"Car tel est notre bon plaisir."*

T HIS SECOND ITALIAN CAMPAIGN of the
French was far less successful than the first,
which nine years previously was led personally by
Charles VIII. In place of a Supreme Marshal de
Gié, a Robert de la Marche, a Cleve, a Vendôme,
Luxembourg, Foix, Urfé and other renowned leaders
who shone around the Sovereign, only a few incon-
sequential counts and minor noblemen agreed to
join La Trémoille's ranks; instead of the countless
millions in minted coin with which the cities through
which Charles had marched had saved themselves
from being sacked; instead of the booty of wonderful paintings, gems, jewellery, brocades and lapis
lazuli with which he had laden his train of 20,000
mules—never mind that soon afterwards, together
with his other effects, he lost it all to the Italians at
the Battle of Fornovo—instead of all that, money
flowed very sparingly into La Trémoille's coffers,
and on his second campaign the Marshal was barely
able to send to Paris anything of note in the way

of paintings, jewels, fabrics, alabaster statues, or to exact due tributes from the people for his Sovereign in Paris, whose express wish and command it was that he should.

The Marshal had in addition spent many months in sharking up the necessary forces, and it was already high summer before he was able to set off on his campaign. He marched through Lombardy, crossed the Apennines and entered Tuscany. While his army, in ostrich-plumed helmets, holding aloft swaying colours, struggled towards Romagna in clouds of dust to the rattle of kettledrums, he himself, accompanied by a suite of noblemen, rode into Florence, where he planned to spend a few days before catching up with his troops with redoubled speed afterwards.

Since, on account of the sparse French forces, there could be no talk of the 120,000 gold pieces, or anything approaching that sum, which the town had at one time yielded to Charles VIII; and since the Marshal, who had to content himself with fleecing the smaller towns, was more than glad the province had so much as let him step on its territory, he decided to concentrate on the purchase of objects of art.

Da Vinci's workshop was recommended to him particularly highly. La Trémoille, who personally found art a terrible bore and had never heard of da Vinci before, decided to pay the great painter a visit, especially since it chimed well with Louis' express wish and command.

Da Vinci was the natural son of a nobleman, Ser Piero, who originally came from the small town of Vinci but had later moved to Florence. After residing for a while in Milan, Venice and elsewhere, da Vinci again ended up in Florence in the house of his father, who was still alive at the time.

It was early morning when La Trémoille set out on his visit, and the high towers of the stately houses, which loomed over the town in their hundreds and gave it the appearance of a factory with numerous chimney stacks, still cast long shadows.

La Trémoille was accompanied by numerous members of his suite: two Donatis, related to Dante and ardent art enthusiasts, although they understood precious little of it; a Buondelmonte, an Alberighi and a Calfucci, the cream of Florentine youth, falling over one another to prove themselves worthy cicerones of the moment. A crowd of idlers followed the cavalcade. The young Florentine noblemen felt flattered to be seen in the company of the strangers, nevertheless the cries issuing from the crowd, which was busy going about its business in the cool of the morning as the riders, swaying in their saddles, their arms akimbo, rode past proudly at walking pace, were closer to curses than any kind of approbation. The point being that the political pendulum of the town had lately swung towards the demotic; the Medici had been ousted and the prevailing attitude towards foreign noblemen, from wheresoever they originated, was as resentful as against their own.

After leaving behind the mob, the dirt and the hustle and bustle of the marketplace, the riders finally reached the quieter, more select regions of the town, and as they drew nearer to Leonardo's house they became aware of string and wind music issuing from it as though there was a celebration in progress. It was a dance tune, which was being played and sung; all the same the laughter, the cries and stamping of the merrymakers' feet stopped as soon as they heard the clatter of hoofs, and by

the time the riders reached the house all the voices within had gone quiet.

The house, constructed of small unhewn stones, was dominated by a watchtower close on 150 feet high. White doves nested in the embrasures of its lower reaches; round its top falcons circled. Washing hung on lines strung out on the galleries. At a distance of about fifteen paces rose the next tower; it was rather narrow but about 180 feet in height, and there were more such towers dotted about the immediate vicinity. Practically the whole of Florence was hemmed in by these towers, disproportionately high in comparison with the houses, many of which had begun to lean over, others to crumble; some however were so high that they appeared like pillars propping up the firmament, which without them would surely have caved in as a consequence of the interminable feuding of the inhabitants. Numerous screeching falcons hovered around them as around clifftops.

After surveying the house and its defences, the Marshal and his followers dismounted and were about to step in when a number of men with musical instruments under their arms emerged from it. Evidently they were the same ones who had just been playing. Among them were also two people, one dressed as a street performer, the other as a tightrope walker.

They squeezed through the doorway past the noblemen and vanished into the open. The stillness into which the house was now plunged was in sharp contrast to the erstwhile cheerfulness. However, the visitors were soon surrounded by a number of servants, and on top of the steep wooden steps which led into the interior appeared Leonardo himself.

Ser Piero's bastard son was forty-five to fifty years old, a tall, handsome man sporting a long beard. He spoke and carried himself with dignity and utmost ease. Accustomed to the society of warlords and princes, he descended a few steps with perfect equanimity.

"My dear sir," La Trémoille said, doffing his hat and beginning to mount the steps, "I am the Marshal of the King of France, and would beg that you extend to me, and by implication to my Sovereign, the honour of being welcomed in your house."

Leonardo replied in grammatically faultless, though heavily Italianate, French:

"My Lord"—La Trémoille was the Viscount of Thouars and held the principality of Talmond; it was more important for an artist to know him and men of his ilk than all the laws of anatomy—"my Lord, the honour and good fortune are entirely mine to greet one of the most renowned commanders of chivalric France. How is His Majesty?"

"The King is full well, as far as I know," La Trémoille said, entering with his suite the upper floor and surveying with admiration the apertures, characteristic of Florentine stately homes, through which, in case of attack, molten pitch was poured on the heads of people down below. "And you, my dear sir?" he continued. "How do things stand with you?"

"Excellently well," Leonardo replied, throwing open a door leading to a small hall. "Though I look in the keen eye of the god of War himself, I hope I may nonetheless enquire after his wellbeing."

"I too," La Trémoille replied as he and his suite entered the hall and let their eyes glide admiringly over the pitch pots sunk in the blue and white mosaic of the floor, "could not feel better. What gives me the greatest pleasure, however, is to make the acquaintance of a painter who puts into shade not only Zeuxis, Protogenes and Apelles, but the fearsome Vulcan himself."

"Which I, however, on account of the legendary griminess of the man on whom Your Excellency has placed horns, must regard as a questionable compliment," Leonardo replied.

The Marshal, who'd learnt the compliments he paid to the painter from one of his priests, had never heard of Vulcan's griminess, nor of the adultery of his wife, Aphrodite, with the god of War. The Marshal had no idea to what sooty husband and to what lady the artist referred, and whether he should perceive it as a flattery, or whether Leonardo was simply poking fun at him. He therefore cast him a sharp look and said:

"With respect, my dear sir, I've no idea what you're talking about! And even if I did, I wouldn't tell you, because a gentleman is no idle chatterbox. Let us therefore speak of other things. But allow me first to introduce you to the noblemen who do me the high favour of following me into the field."

"Nothing would please me more," Leonardo said.

"Well, they are as follows," the Marshal went on: "the Counts of Villeneuve, de Goutaut-Biron and de Jarnac, as well as Messieurs Costé de Triquerville, du Plessis, de Chauvelin and de Bridieu, then there is the Viscount of Châteaudun and the young gentleman de Bougainville, the nephew of the renowned French General du Val de Bonneval. No doubt the Florentine noblemen who've taken it upon themselves to conduct me to you need no introduction."

"Gentlemen," Leonardo said, "I am your devoted servant," and the cavaliers whom the Marshal mentioned bowed and remained standing, leaning on their swords in the attitude of people who were ever ready to step out of the way of anyone who should go past them. Only no one did, and an awkward pause occurred. For, after acknowledging the honour and pleasure of having made one another's acquaintance, no one knew for a time what to say next. In the meantime servants appeared offering refreshments, and La Trémoille, casting a glance around the hall, said:

"Would you now, my dear sir, give us the pleasure of being permitted to see your workshop?"

"My workshop?" Leonardo answered. "But you are in my workshop now, Monseigneur."

This sparsely furnished hall, curtained off at the far end, was indeed Leonardo's workshop. A few empty chairs stood near the walls and on a sideboard lay a couple of letters, poems, sketches and drawings of fortifications, canals and the like. That was all.

For Leonardo was not only one of the most extraordinary, but perhaps for that very reason one of the most absent-minded people of his time. There are dozens of paintings which are considered more or less his, to which however he contributed no more than a few touches. Their completion he left to others.

He attempted all manner of sculpting in bronze, stone and baked clay, but finished hardly anything, and the greater part of what he did finish was later destroyed by time. He had no end of projects on the go, practically all of which he later abandoned to preoccupy himself with anything that took his fancy, rather than with the matter in hand. Perhaps he realized that in truth nothing could ever be accomplished fully. It is certain that nothing, or almost nothing, is ever accomplished to the end, and the little that has been may, in the last analysis, be a delusion.

"How can that be, my dear sir," La Trémoille exclaimed, "you say this is your workshop? Upon my soul, I imagined it to be something different! When I leave a battlefield, which in a sense is my workshop, you would own that there is something of fine art in the severed heads, arms and legs which lie scattered about! So where are your paintings, your sculptures, the sketches that you are presently working on?"

"At the moment I'm not working on anything like that," Leonardo replied. "Or, to be more precise, I've not yet had the opportunity to resume my artistic endeavours. For the last two years I was the engineer of the Duke of Valentinois, and I've just returned from the Pisa encampment where I was charged with designing siege engines and other military equipment for the Florentine army. Since then I've been preoccupied with other pursuits."

"And if I may enquire, what would those pursuits be?"

"I have been taking an interest in music, anatomy and a little in philosophy," Leonardo responded. "I've resolved to depict the essence of love in verses and, in order to probe into the anatomical origins of the same, I too have had arms and legs lying around in my workshop—in short, I dissected the bodies of two women. The only thing is, I've failed to discover anything of note."

"I could have told you that in advance, my dear sir," the Marshal said. "How was it at all possible that you expected to find something precisely where the only thing that one can really hope to find is lack of will! For, if even the women of Paris are as weak as water, what can you expect of two dead Italian women! Well, and what did you do next?"

"I gave the whole thing up."

"That you ought not to have done either," the Marshal remarked. "Instead you should have followed the example of all mankind, which has been preoccupied with precisely the same investigation since Adam and Eve and has still not given up. For, upon my soul, you've stumbled upon a worthy subject, if only by chance! So what are you engaged upon instead?"

"I'm sketching a ship," Leonardo said, "in which one can go to the bottom of the sea, and another in which one can rise into the air."

"Bless my soul," the Marshal exclaimed, "that has much more promise about it, it seems to me. Not that I would exchange such ships for a good horse, but one could persuade one's enemies to board them so that they'd either drown in the deep or fall from the sky and break their necks. Also that Valentino of yours"—meaning Cesare Borgia—"would have been grateful to you for such an invention. You ought to have presented him with one such while you were still in his service."

"My investigations," Leonardo said, "led me, after my enquiries into the density and flow of water and air, to other things, and for a few days I was preoccupied with the weight of God."

"Well, well, how much does He weigh then?" asked the Marshal, who was beginning to suspect more and more that he was dealing with someone who was making fun of him, and he therefore resolved to adopt an equally derisive tone. "What conclusions did you manage to reach then, may I ask, my dear Sir Flibbertigibbet?"

"None, of course," Leonardo replied. "Nor did I seek to reach a conclusion. For who could possibly reach a conclusion of that sort, especially with regard to God! I merely enjoyed immersing myself in contemplating Him. That's all."

"And," La Trémoille asked, furrowing his brows, "did you do nothing else?"

"On the contrary. I studied the nature of water nymphs, wood spirits, griffins and dragons, not to mention unicorns and other rare beings."

"Very well," the Marshal said, "that is good and very useful indeed! But do you investigate the specifics of the more common animals?"

"No," Leonardo said, "because they're already well known as it is."

"You think so? Tell me then, if you please, how many legs has a fly, for instance."

"A fly?" Leonardo responded, "Four, naturally!"

"No," the Marshal said, "six. I knew you'd get it wrong."

"Monseigneur," Leonardo said, "a fly has only four legs and no more."

"And I, my dear sir," the Marshal retorted, "assure you that it has six, and I won't give up a single one of them."

"In a book that I wrote myself in an idle moment in my youth and which deals with various animals, I stated precisely that a fly has four…"

"Six, I tell you, sir! But so as not to make a spectacle of ourselves in the eyes of the world, which are directed on us as though we were falling out over something the truth of which every schoolboy can verify, I will, with your permission, catch a fly and provide you with the opportunity of counting its legs. Monsieur de Bougainville! You are the youngest of my entourage. Pray, be so kind as to catch a fly for us!"

The young man whom the Marshal had addressed was at first nonplussed by the order he had received. But he soon took a grip of himself and replied in all good humour, "Your wish is my command, Monseigneur! It is as good as done!"

"On the shoulder of Monsieur de Bridieu," the Marshal said, rather severely however, because he could not possibly tolerate that a command of his should not be taken seriously, "I can see a fly sitting just now. Stand quite still, Monsieur de Bridieu!" And Monsieur de Bougainville began to approach Monsieur de Bridieu to apprehend the fly. However, sensing Monsieur de Bougainville's proximity, it rose from Monsieur de Bridieu's shoulder and began to buzz around the room, pursued by the rest of the suite, who hit out at it with their plumed hats. Finally it disappeared behind the curtain at the far end of the hall, which Bougainville pulled aside.

A fantastic effulgence greeted his eyes. At the first instant he believed it to be a flame, or the radiance of jewels. Only the luminance came from the perfectly flat surface of a picture, propped up at an angle on a chair and painted in a novel art on wood or metal, its brilliance enhanced not merely by egg white but certain rare oils. It could have been about two feet by three or a little bigger, was in a simple frame and depicted a young woman in a silver-grey frock with sleeves of Indian yellow. The woman, whose face was turned towards the viewer, looked a little sideways to the left, where Bougainville stood, and she smiled. Her smile was enchanting and mysterious, as if glimpsed through fine shadows or a veil, though it exuded a luminosity which dazzled the eyes; and in the background, where sky-blue streams wound around huge mountains, the azure glow was more enchanting than the lustre of paradise.

Bougainville saw the woman only for a short space of time, because the very next moment he felt the artist's firm arm around his shoulders and the curtain before him was pulled back again.

"What was that?" Bougainville asked in confusion.

"Nothing," Leonardo said as he led the young man back into the centre of the hall. "A picture, that's all."

"A picture?" the Marshal asked. "What kind of a picture? May I see it?"

"It is not finished," Leonardo said. "I'm still working on it every now and again."

"Still, could I have a quick look…"

"I'd rather you didn't, Monseigneur. It is woefully unfinished. It's a mere trifle."

"And would you sell it? It is the express wish and command of my King…"

"Perhaps. However, I'm not going to sell it before it's completed, and I don't know…"

"You will find," the Marshal said, "the price quite to your liking. I could impose a small levy on some neighbouring town."

"But who is the woman?" Bougainville exclaimed. "What's her name?"

Leonardo paused for a second, then said, "Gioconda."

"And who is she?"

"Oh, no one of consequence."

"Sir," Bougainville insisted, "may I be permitted another question…"

"You may not, Monsieur!"

So ended this essentially fruitless, but as will shortly become evident, very fraught meeting. The matter of the fly and how many legs it has became a total irrelevance. The Marshal, after exchanging a few more words with the artist about other affairs, withdrew, left the house and mounted his horse, and there was nothing for it but for Bougainville to follow him and his people.

PHILIPPE DE BOUGAINVILLE, who came from a family which about 200 years later became very famous on account of a major sea voyage which one of his namesakes performed, was twenty-three years old when he agreed to march to Italy under the banners of La Trémoille. The impression which the painting of the unknown woman had made on him was quite extraordinary, and on the return journey he questioned the Florentines closely as to who she might be. The young people replied that they didn't really know a Gioconda, except that, judging by her name, she could be the wife or relative of a gentleman by the name of Giocondo; and there was only one such in Florence, a certain Francesco del Giocondo who resided in the vicinity of Bargello. The only thing being that he was a widower. "So, if the picture, which you had no opportunity of seeing, is that of his wife, or more accurately one of his wives, because he was married three times, she is well and truly dead, and we have no knowledge of any other relative of his going by that name." Moreover, he was hardly ever to be seen in public. He was of course a nobleman, but though he held a number of civic posts, he kept himself to himself by and large.

It struck young Bougainville as totally improbable that Leonardo would have painted a woman who was no longer alive. Yet he found out from other sources too in the course of the same day, which he spent exclusively on his enquiries, that Giocondo's three wives had died, the last of them—Mona Lisa di Antonio Maria di Noldo Gherardini, a relative of Cesare Borgia's private secretary Agapito Gherardini—of the plague in 1501, and that Giocondo had not married again.

Bougainville, who immediately concluded that the painting with which—or more precisely its model, with whom—he had fallen madly in love was another woman, resolved to make her acquaintance and decided, despite the offensive manner in which Leonardo had concluded the discussion with him, to pay him another visit.

Much to his surprise, as Bougainville reached the Via Ghibellina and approached da Vinci's house, he once more heard music issuing from it, and it was again a dance tune which people played and sang, yet on this occasion it did not cease as the young man proceeded. Evidently, as he was alone and on foot, no one had noticed him. He stepped into the entrance hall, mounted the stairs and stopped on the landing.

The music came from the same hall in which Leonardo had greeted the Marshal the day before.

After hesitating a little, Bougainville pushed the door open and saw—

The curtain, which he himself had pulled aside yesterday, was now fully open, and Leonardo, his back to the door, a box (such as artisans carry their tools in on a strap over their shoulder) filled with paints on the floor beside him and a small bundle of paintbrushes in his right hand, was sitting on a chair looking at Gioconda's picture, which was propped up on another chair in front of him. This manner of painting appeared most makeshift in character; besides, a number of musicians, evidently the same as yesterday, filled the air with music. Also the two gleemen were about, dancing and beating their tambourines.

The spectacle was all the more remarkable because it was not enacted before Leonardo's eyes, rather at his back, so that he could not see the musicians, his eyes resting on the image of the woman alone. Also, he was not doing anything; instead he sat motionless in a peculiarly tense, almost provocatively unnatural posture, with just the fingers of his left hand beating in time with the music.

Bougainville, as soon as he again beheld the astonishing lustre of the picture, also came to a complete standstill, until the musicians noticed him and broke off their song.

The artist turned around sharply and a few seconds later sprang to his feet.

He was more than taken aback to see Bougainville, and his face went red.

"My dear sir," he spoke after a pause, "to what do I owe the honour of this second visit?" He threw the brushes into the paintbox, and with a majestic sweep of his arm dismissed the musicians and the two gleemen. "Please pardon the presence of these people," he added hastily. "But I was not prepared for visitors. I decided just recently to try my hand at painting again, but my work bores me, and these good people help me to forget myself." (He had evidently forgotten that they must have been noticed yesterday too.) "*Via, via!*" he called out, and the minstrels, who had already picked up their belongings, left the hall. He was just about to draw the curtain shut when Bougainville rushed up to him and fell across his arm. The young man moved so softly and swiftly that his feet hardly seemed to touch the ground.

"Don't!" he implored with a movement which by its grace and youthful passion touched the artist deeply. "Allow me, Messere, to enjoy for at least a few minutes the sight of this wonderful woman, who has occupied my mind since yesterday to the exclusion of everything else. I'll admit to you openly that she is the reason behind my present visit. Otherwise I'd not have had the audacity to encroach upon your valuable time. You may consider me childish, but I don't have the ability to draw a distinction between the beauty of an artwork and its model. Who is this model? I beg you, Messere, to name her! Yesterday you declared she's the wife of Francesco del Giocondo, only…"

"What was that?" Leonardo interrupted him in surprise. "I said she was Giocondo's wife?"

"Yes, of course! You mentioned her name…"

"Ser Francesco's wife?"

"That's right."

"One moment!" Leonardo exclaimed. "I never said he was her husband! All I said was she's Gioconda!"

"Quite so, quite so! Only Mona Lisa is dead. She has been for the last two years, and Ser Francesco's other two wives have been dead for years too."

"What, did he have two more wives?"

"That's right. Mona Vanna and Mona Bice."

"Well, well! I never knew that," Leonardo muttered under his breath. "But how do you know all that? And what precisely do you want from me?— Would you at least do me the honour of taking a seat!" And he brought up two chairs.

"Messer Leonardo," Bougainville said as he sat down and laid his plumed hat over his knee, "I beg you, tell me who the lady is! I implore you! Could she be the wife of someone other than Ser Francesco? Is she one of his relatives who lives in another town?

Or is she your own mistress and you simply don't want to say who she is?"

"Young man," Leonardo said with dignity, "if she were my paramour, it would have been my pleasure to introduce her to you. You would have made a beautiful couple, and I personally, even if it cost me dearly, would have left no stone unturned to behold such a couple. For in the main one sees only very ugly couples. I'm afraid though that you will be unable to make the acquaintance which you so ardently desire. You said yourself that Ser Francesco's wife was dead, didn't you?"

"Well then, is this painting that of Gioconda?"

"Yes."

"And Mona Lisa is really dead?"

"No doubt about it."

"Then," Bougainville exclaimed, convulsed with pain, "nothing is left for me but to weep on her grave! For, just when I thought I'd found her, I had already lost her long ago. But you, Messere, who knew her, had spoken to her, had breathed the same air, tell me all you know about her, tell me absolutely everything in the minutest detail, and out of this ether I will fashion me a picture which will be more wonderful than yours!"

"Oh," Leonardo said, raising his eyebrows, "I knew her only fleetingly, and the picture of the woman before you is neither her nor anyone else. The truth is, even had I wanted to paint her, it would have immediately turned into the likeness of someone else. After all, one always paints women who never exist, and the same goes for women one really loves. But of course it is possible that this painting bears a certain likeness to her. It is not unthinkable that this Gioconda and the other one… that, in view of the matching names, certain memories… The reason I've called her Gioconda is because she smiles, for in Italian the word means the happy or the smiling one. Mona Lisa was someone else. But in the event it would not have been quite outside the realms of possibility that, precisely for that reason, the memories of the other one, the real person, had found their way into the crafted picture, had displaced the imagined outlines… For none of us knows what it is that speaks for us, writes for us, moves our brush, or how many lives, long since passed away, still continue to respire within us! If the truth be known…"

Bougainville had got to his feet. "Had I not been sure," he said, stepping a little to the right so that the eyes of the painting, looking slightly to the left, met his, "had I not been convinced that the woman, whose likeness I took this picture to be, was dead, had it not been absolutely certain that she'd been dead and buried for years, I could have sworn that she looks more alive than many a living one. It is quite unthinkable that these eyes no longer see, that this bosom no longer heaves, that the smile on her lips is not a live, but an immortal one! I—"

"The smile," Leonardo interrupted him as he put one foot on the paintbox and, leaning forward, picked up a few brushes which he then let drop one by one, "the smile is not immortal, it's merely unfinished, that's all."

"It is wonderful," Bougainville said.

"No, it is not. Women are without a doubt the most perfect creations, and when they smile they are at their most perfect. A smile is the expression of perfection par excellence. All that has been shifted, is distorted, all that is in a state of rest, smiles. But nothing can be more worthy of a dismissive smile than the unfinished depiction of perfection, and despite my efforts to capture it, the smile of this woman has eluded me. Every smile is a mystery, not only of itself, but in every other respect too. But I have no clue to this mystery. I know not what she is smiling at. You are no doubt surprised, sir, to find me surrounded by musicians and gleemen. Well, I allowed myself to be persuaded that this lady could raise a smile at the sight of people dancing. They were charged, so to speak, to entertain the painting and to evoke an expression in it which I myself was incapable of doing. For myself, I find the expression on the picture absurd. The smile of a real woman, be she the commonest one of all, is in any event more accomplished than any attempt to depict it even by the greatest painter in the world. Perhaps the point is that there is no perfection in things artistic. I'm sure there isn't. Only the real is perfect." And after a pause he added, "Not until the woman in this painting becomes real will it be said that she really smiles."

"Well," Bougainville muttered, "she's real enough for me. The agony I'm going through that she's no longer alive exceeds the grief over the loss of the most beautiful *inamoratas*..."

"So you've fallen in love with this painting?"

"Not with the painting," Bougainville said. "With the lady."

"Which, at least in this case, comes to the same thing."

"For you it does, Messere," Bougainville said. "But not for me." And he stared into the void. "However," he finally added, pulling himself together, "it's pointless going over what has been lost. Besides, I fear I have exceeded my welcome. Still, I know you will pardon my intrusion, my questions and my madness. Put it down to the dreams, yours and mine, that they can be far more authentic than life itself."

And without giving the painting another glance, he bowed and left the hall, suppressing his emotions.

MONA VANNA AND MONA BICE del Giocondo, as well as a child daughter of Ser Francesco, were buried at the outer wall of Santa Maria Novella, Mona Lisa, however, in Santa Croce; in fact, on account of her family's nobility, within the church itself, in the right aisle.

The tomb was in the wall between the so-called Baroncelli Chapel and the entrance to the sacristy. A marble plate, framed in the style of the times and bearing an inscription in Latin which Bougainville did not understand, was sunk into the stonework. It was about midday when, accompanied by a servant who carried a garland of dark red roses, he entered the church. The Mass that was in progress was for late risers, the "scented Mass" as it was known, attended by richly turned-out and heavily perfumed nobility who actually came only to see and be seen, to criticize, to laugh and to gossip. As for the priest and what went on at the altar, no one bothered in the slightest.

The spectacle of the elegant, happy-go-lucky, chattering crowd filled Bougainville with foreboding; he noticed the looks which the ladies cast him. Shoving aside their escorts, who could not be induced to move out of the way, and ignoring their protests, he allowed himself to be conducted to Mona Lisa's tomb.

He crowned it with the garland of roses. Then he stepped back and stood still in deep contemplation.

His intention had been to seek peace and remain at the grave for as long as possible right up to the moment of his departure, never letting the deceased out of his mind. Now that he was standing before the tomb, however, he was suddenly overcome by a strange sensation of not knowing at all what had led him to the place or what he actually sought.

Looking at the painting, he could not imagine she was dead. At her grave, he could not imagine that she still lived for him in any shape or form. That he could have crowned the tomb of a complete stranger with roses struck him suddenly as a tasteless imposition, an inexcusable intrusion into the personal affairs of others; had he just then been confronted by one of her relatives, or even her husband, he would

have been at a loss what to say. The red of the roses offended his sight. He turned away and let his eyes wander over the ornate walls, the rich hangings and the long rows of triangular wooden shields covered in deeply tanned leather, hanging from the brightly coloured roof beams.

He cast a cursory glance at the Baroncelli Chapel. Here too, tombs, tapestries, shields. Yet as he turned back, it occurred to him that the wall between the chapel and the church proper was unusually slender. After he had entered the nave of the church, as far as he could tell, there could be no coffin in this thin wall to the left of the entrance. To the right, however, was Mona Lisa's tomb.

Still farther to the right, adjacent to the passageway which led to the sacristy, was yet another tomb from much earlier times, but set into the very substantial wall of the church. Ser Francesco's wife was behind the plate of the tomb, though the wall was at most only one and a half cubits thick, with the chapel adjacent to it.

Bougainville looked at this wall and could not comprehend how the corpse could have been accommodated within it; could it have been placed in an upright position, which was however most unlikely and would have gone against all accepted practice? Or perhaps the coffin was under the floor and only the memorial plate attached to the wall? But then the inscribed plate would have been in the floor too.

Bougainville shuddered and his heart, as though someone had reached out and laid his hand on it, missed a beat. He took a couple of steps into the chapel, but turned back and his eyes ran desperately over the wall.

It seemed impossible that a full-grown woman could have been buried there, for otherwise the wall would have had to be more than an arm's length thicker. Otherwise there'd be no room for the deceased in it. But if not here, where else was she interred?

It is reasonable that, spiritually disturbed as he was, he had dismissed the woman's death from the very start and considered no other possibility than that she was still alive.

"If someone," a voice in him cried, "does not rest in the grave which properly speaking belongs to him but in which, due to its diminutive dimensions, he would not fit, it follows he is not dead! When an artist works on the portrait of a woman at the sight of which someone standing just two paces away has to gasp for breath at how real she looks, be the artist even as great as Leonardo, the likeness could not stem from the realm of the imagination alone, and it is therefore impossible that she's been dead these past two years! When he says she no longer serves him as a model he lies, and when that Giocondo claims he's put up a tomb for her it's only to deceive everyone! I do not know on what grounds the two of them have decided to conceal the existence of this wonderful creature, I do not know why her husband is hiding her and where he's hiding her. No doubt in some lair in his house in a state of unbecoming captivity. Why? She must have been unfaithful to him. A man who, instead of killing the wife who deceived him, punishes her by burying her alive, a man who is so cowardly as not to own to her and his own shame, but who repays her by tormenting her in secret—she had to deceive such a man as soon as she realized what type of person she was dealing with. There's no other explanation. And he, ghoul that he is, is now seeking to avenge himself on the misguided creature for the calamity into which he himself had precipitated her!"

He promptly decided to do all that was possible to liberate her. To confide his findings to the municipal authorities was not an option for him. Those people would not believe or comprehend the enormity of what had taken place before their very eyes, and would laugh in his face. And he was not inclined, especially after the painter himself had led him by the nose, to be the laughing stock of the world. He also rejected the idea of confiding in La Trémoille, who found himself entangled in the net of Italian politics. The best he could think of was simply to turn to his friends and, with their and their friends' help, to break into Giocondo's house and set the unfortunate woman free.

Nevertheless, he said to himself that before he undertook this course of action he must be absolutely sure of his case, even more sure than he was already. There always was the chance, however slim, that she lay buried in the coffin.

He therefore decided personally to put his conjectures to the test and in the night open up the tomb.

He spent the afternoon in the grip of warring emotions, partly imagining the unfortunate circumstances of his beloved, partly in a state of euphoria that she was yet alive and that he would see and speak to her. Then again he was seized by the fear that her grave was in fact real. The day seemed to him to drag on for ever, and as soon as dusk descended he was already in Santa Croce, accompanied by two of his servants with the necessary tools concealed under their coats. The three of them stayed out of sight behind a side altar till the church was locked shut, then they came forth and proceeded to open the tomb.

By the light of some candle stumps which they took from one of the altars, they wrenched the memorial plaque from the wall and behind it exposed the bricked-in entrance to the tomb. They hacked at it, shoved the rubble aside and shone a light into the interior.

Bougainville had not been wrong. The tomb was empty.

I T IS POSSIBLE that in times gone by it had con-
tained the body of a stillborn child or one that
had died soon after birth, because the space was no
more than a cubit deep. Ser Francesco had purchased
the tomb and had made it known to all that it was
the resting place of his wife. Amid the universal
panic which then raged on account of the plague,
and since no one would have dared to witness the
interment, the deception went unnoticed and no
suspicions were aroused.

However, Bougainville, who wanted to play it
completely safe, ordered even the flagstones in front
of the tomb to be lifted and the ground turned over.
But nothing was found.

After he had restored everything more or less
as it was originally, his flunkeys turned to one of
the doors of the church and began to force it open.
People of their ilk could put their hand to anything,
and in no time at all the lock gave way.

When Bougainville emerged into the purple of

the night on the great square before the church, it was about ten o'clock. He went straight to Leonardo's.

The house was locked shut; it took quite a lot of banging before the door was finally opened. The artist had already retired for the night. Leonardo's father, the old notary, and the artist's stepmother Lucrezia, his half-brothers and their wives as well as the always idle Francesco da Vinci, who also resided in the house, having been roused from their early slumbers by the commotion, emerged half dressed in the entrance hall in the light provided by the servants, and took Bougainville, who rushed past them to Leonardo's room without taking the slightest notice of them, for a complete and utter lunatic. Leonardo came to the very same conclusion when Bougainville declared to him that he was no less of a scoundrel than Ser Francesco, because Mona Lisa was not dead but was kept prisoner in inhuman conditions. Sitting up in bed and rubbing his eyes in bewilderment, Leonardo stared at the young man, who seemed to be beside himself, asking Bougainville again and again as to what led him to such an outlandish conclusion.

"First-hand evidence!" Bougainville cried out. "First-hand evidence that I procured personally! You, Messer Leonardo, are a gallows-bird and a liar to boot! Because you wanted to make me believe that Mona Lisa was dead. But not a bit of it. It hasn't even entered her head to be dead!"

"She is not dead?" Leonardo exclaimed. "Pray tell me, what is she then?"

"She's alive!" Bougainville cried. "What else can she be! She's not in her tomb!"

"Ah," Leonardo exclaimed, "she's not in her tomb! How do you pretend to know that?"

"I've opened it!" Bougainville bellowed.

"You did what?" Leonardo said. "You opened her tomb?"

"That's right! And it was empty. So, tell me where she is! Tell me the dreadful plot of which she is the victim! Tell me all or by God," he cried, drawing his dagger, "I'll stab you right away in your own bed!"

After a moment Leonardo threw his blanket aside, got up and, his eyes fixed on Bougainville, approached him directly. He was, according to how people slept at the time, completely naked; his massive beard hid his chest, but the rest of his body exposed an unusually well-developed muscular frame. Bougainville involuntarily took a step back.

"Young man," Leonardo said, "just a moment!" And with a swift, very gentle movement he raised Bougainville's right eyelid.

"What was that for?" Bougainville exclaimed.

"Nothing," Leonardo said, reached for a dressing gown, which lay across a chair, and put it on. "Nothing at all, young man. Put that thing away! So, you are convinced you know that Ser Francesco's wife is not in her tomb? Where would she be then?"

"That," Bougainville cried, "is what I came to ask you! Where is she? You know it! You must know it, because before she vanished off the face of the earth you painted her! Is she still in Ser Francesco's house? Why is he hiding her? Or perhaps she wants to remain hidden herself? I don't think so! So why does Giocondo conceal her existence? Has she been unfaithful to him, but he lacked the courage to kill her and is tormenting her instead? Who was her lover? Out with it! Out with it, I say!"

Leonardo looked at the young man and said at last, "Because you stand before me brandishing your dagger, you imagine you can make me talk. Be assured that it would be the simplest thing in the world to disarm you and send you head over heels down the steps. However, your state—not to mention the mental aberration of which you are a victim—excuses you to a degree. I could, for instance, answer your questions, provided of course you had the right to put them to me. However, it is hardly necessary that I should. You answer them yourself, and I couldn't have made a better job of it myself even if I'd wanted to. Let me sum up briefly: you pay me a visit in the company of your Marshal. By chance you catch sight of the picture of a woman who does not exist, but with whom you nevertheless fall in love. You take this woman to be Ser Francesco del Giocondo's wife, who died two years ago. However, you cannot reconcile yourself to the thought that she may be dead. You claim to have gone through her tomb and found it empty. As a result you conclude that she's still alive. You make surmises as to her whereabouts from which it is plainly obvious that in your fevered imagination you've already settled that question. Would it be any use for me to try to explain to you that Mona Lisa is dead? That Giocondo is not hiding her? That I hadn't painted her, that she had not deceived him? Come to think of it, she may really have been unfaithful to him. There are rumours about that her lover was Amerigo Capponi, the son of Ser Piero, to whom Florence owes so much. When your King Charles imposed unfair obligations on our city, which he had invaded, Ser Piero tore up the agreement and negotiated a more advantageous one. But even this, I fear, is only grist to your mill. Because you will obviously take it as given that the, in your eyes, most beautiful woman in Florence had no other friend save the son of the foremost Etruscan nobleman. In truth, however, what is there for you in it? The matter is years old. Still, you're as unlikely to believe me in this as in anything else. Therefore, as far as I'm concerned you might as well stick to your version. She lives, her husband, whom she'd deceived, keeps her hidden and I, I have painted her. Are you satisfied now?"

"Your reasons," retorted Bougainville, who had listened to him with sparkling eyes, "for confirming my surmises—what am I saying? My convictions!—are of no interest to me, my dear sir! Whether you think I'm mad or not, you do not deny that Mona Lisa may still be alive, do you?"

"What would be the point," Leonardo said, "of me insisting on anything else?"

"And is this Messer Capponi still her lover?"

"I ought not," Leonardo said, shrugging his shoulders, "have told you that. If, however, you can in the event persuade yourself that it is feasible for a woman, while being held in captivity by her husband, still to contrive to have a lover, have it your way. Women—you will concede—are very resourceful, and will use every ploy to achieve their ends, and the lovers of hapless women have it in them to be extraordinarily faithful. The two are still very much in love. And now, I'd be most grateful to you if you would be so good as to leave me. I still have a mind to snatch a couple more hours' sleep. That apart, I'm pretty sure you will give me the pleasure of paying me another visit before too long. Don't hesitate therefore to inconvenience me, but at least spare Giocondo and Capponi, on whom I have, incidentally, drawn a bill recently, or something of the kind. Speaking for myself, I'm used to being imposed upon. And so, goodbye!"

Bougainville, who had put the dagger under his arm, stood still for a few more seconds, and it seemed he was about to say something.

"I expected as much," was all he finally muttered.

And, without taking his leave, he turned sharp on his heels and left the house.

W HEN BOUGAINVILLE RETURNED, a number of La Trémoille's noblemen were still up. They sat in the house of a certain Fifante, drinking their fill in the company of a few girls and singing in full voice, "*Mignonne, allons voir,*" and, "*Ha! belle blonde.*"

"Gentlemen," Bougainville said, joining them, "please excuse me for interrupting your merry-making. Only I need your help in a very important matter."

The singers fell silent, but one of the girls, just then being tickled by Monsieur de Pierredon, who hadn't noticed Bougainville come in, screeched out. When, however, Pierredon realized that in the ensuing silence all eyes were turned on him he changed tack, and from being amiable turned vicious by delivering the girl a loud smack across her face. She sprang to her feet in a rage and dashed out of the room.

Bougainville, his eyes aflame, looked from one to the other.

"Well, my dear sir," the Vicomte de Châteaudun finally asked, "what is it all about? I hope you will have the goodness to tell us."

"A lady…" Bougainville began.

"Naturally, a lady!" Monsieur de Chauvelin exclaimed. "Only what is the problem with this lady?"

"She is being held captive in this city in demeaning conditions. Allow me to describe the circumstances which have led me to discover her unfortunate plight. It might suffice for you to know that this lady is very young, very beautiful and very unfortunate. I consider it my duty to come to her aid and I'm counting on your support, gentlemen. Let us break into the house, search it and free the lady!"

Bougainville's proposal was immediately taken up with exclamations of joy. The noblemen were in any case aware that they were regarded not as masters, like in the times of Charles VIII nine years previously, but were merely tolerated. Bougainville's proposal offered a most welcome opportunity to change this state of affairs. "Monsieur de Bougainville," the noblemen called out, "that is good! That is excellent,

Monsieur de Bougainville! Your proposal is one of the best! It will be our pleasure to put our persons at your disposal! We are delighted to be of service to you! Long live Bougainville! Upon my honour, young as he is, he's also one of the noblest men! He takes after Monsieur de Bonneval, his uncle! He follows completely in his footsteps!"

They did not make any further enquiries as to the circumstances or even the name of the lady to whom they were ready to extend their help; instead they called for their arms and horses, and a little later the cavalcade, followed by servants, moved with noisy defiance towards Ser Francesco's residence, Bougainville at the head. The entrance to the house and the windows within reach were bombarded with rocks and stones and the door was finally forced open. Shouting and alarm overwhelmed the whole neighbourhood. People, woken from their sleep, began to peer from all the windows, asking what the blazes was going on. A bell began to peal erratically.

Ser Francesco confronted the intruders on the first floor. He was a man of about forty to forty-five years of age, of a respectable appearance, slightly greying, but still possessed of youthful charm. With hardly any clothes on, he was wielding a sword in his hand. Behind him were ranged his servants, armed with bats, rolling pins and skewering irons.

"My dear friends of France," he said, "what gives you the right to break into my house? How dare you break down the door? What do you want here?"

"That, scoundrel that you are," the Count of Jarnac exclaimed, "you are about to find out!" In truth, he himself wasn't sure. However, Bougainville planted himself in front of Giocondo and yelled, "Where's your wife?"

Ser Francesco looked at him in bewilderment.

"That's right!" Bougainville bellowed. "Your wife! Where is she? We want to know!"

"Gentlemen," Ser Francesco said, "who are you that you assume the right to enquire after her? I no longer have a wife. I had three, but they all died."

"That's just not true!" Bougainville insisted. "What I mean is, Mona Vanna and Mona Bice are dead, but not Mona Lisa!"

"How do you know that?" Giocondo exclaimed. "Or, more to the point, what gives you that idea? Did you know her? And besides, how is it you are informed about my family's affairs?"

"As a matter of fact," Bougainville retorted, "I'm excellently well informed! Besides, I've also uncovered things of which others are quite ignorant, for instance that your wife is not at all buried in Santa Croce. What say you to that, my Italian friend, well?"

Giocondo took a couple of steps back; he went red and appeared to have been touched to the quick. "What on earth do you mean?" he finally asked.

"I mean what I mean!" Bougainville bellowed.

"But what makes you so certain?"

"Because I've verified it all myself!"

"What?" Giocondo exclaimed. "You would have…"

"That's right! Not only would I have, I indeed have as a matter of fact! So tell me, where is that wife of yours? Tell me immediately if you don't want me to seek out with the tip of this blade where you've hidden your secret—you villain, that you should have had the audacity to keep such a delightful creature from the eyes of the world, to torment her and even to have her portrait painted!"

For a brief moment Giocondo stood completely motionless, then, all of a sudden, instead of answering, he shoved Bougainville aside, drove his way through the ranks of the noblemen who stood in his way and quickly slid down the banister to the bottom of the stairs.

"Stop!" Bougainville cried.

However Giocondo had already reached the gate of the house and rushed out onto the street, and as Bougainville, who had followed him down the stairs, also reached the gate, Ser Francesco was already in the throng which had gathered in front of the house; and when Bougainville appeared the crowd greeted him with such a hostile howl that he dared not follow the fugitive, who was already out of sight.

In the meantime the French noblemen, having kicked Ser Francesco's servants out of the way, had begun to turn everything in the house upside down. Only there was no trace of Mona Lisa. All that was found in the house on the distaff side were two young, quite pretty servant girls who'd been dragged out of bed naked and, despite their screaming and screeching, were being passed around in triumph till it became painfully obvious that neither of them was the person sought, both subsequently dashing about and wringing their hands between the naked swords of the cavaliers like two disturbed chickens. But the disturbance came to an abrupt and sudden end. Giocondo returned at the head of a party of armed Florentine noblemen whom he had summoned to his aid. The Florentines stormed into the house and the French were hard put to save their skins. In the course of a short engagement during which even a few pistols shots were heard, though fortunately no one sustained any more serious injury than a couple of scratches, the French secured the exit and made their retreat in the face of the enraged mob, which had already filled all the streets and was pelting the unwelcome guests with stones, garbage and rotten vegetables.

WHEN THE SCANDAL which his noblemen had caused reached his ears, La Trémoille fell into a towering rage since his relations with the city authorities, not the most sanguine at the best of times—for he and his followers, far from welcome, were barely tolerated—deteriorated sharply as a consequence. He was obliged despite the late hour to appear before the Signoria, who had also been alerted, to plead for pardon, promising to mete out punishment to the originators of the turmoil, and he upbraided his nobles in the severest terms. Above all, he wanted to establish what was behind this disturbance. Curiously, however, no one seemed to know all of a sudden. The noblemen excused themselves as being drunk. As they hadn't found the woman whom Bougainville was after, they began to suspect whether she ever existed. In any case, they thought it was more prudent not even to mention her, and there was nothing for it but for La Trémoille, who had not established anything coherent, to confine them all under arrest in their quarters. Naturally, Giocondo too hesitated to say anything regarding the true reason for the hullabaloo, and in the event the whole occurrence was looked upon as nothing more than the drunken excesses of some court gallants.

Bougainville, hemmed in by four walls, was, as a result of his failed undertaking, in a state of desperation. The fact that his beloved could not be found was beyond him. But at the same time a new fear began to gnaw at him that Giocondo, now he realized that the cat was out of the bag and that she was indeed being sought, would hold her in even stricter confinement and subject her to ever greater torment.

In his desperation, he finally decided to draw La Trémoille into his confidence. He sent him a message, begging for an interview to discuss a highly urgent matter.

When La Trémoille arrived, Bougainville thanked the Marshal most cordially for having granted him the pleasure of his visit.

"The pleasure, my dear sir," La Trémoille replied as he threw his hat on the table and sank into an easy chair, "the pleasure is certainly not on my side, you can believe me!"

"In that case, Monseigneur," Bougainville said, "I beg you to accept an expression of my profound regret. Above all, I have no idea what the cause of your renewed displeasure towards me is."

"My dear sir," La Trémoille retorted, as he struck his riding crop across his calves, their boot leggings at half-mast, "on my way here, despite my escort, not only was I personally abused by the crowd, but insults were directed against France and the King. The nobility of Florence is up in arms against us and the inhabitants are like a disturbed hornets' nest. Secret assassins have been trying to stab us in the back. The obeisance which I offered the Signoria was as good as ignored, in the night a local patriot hacked off the tail of my piebald flush with its hind-quarters in the stables, and all in all, thanks to the general upheaval, we are in constant danger of quite simply being arrested. What do you say to that? Had I suspected what irresponsible pranks you, my dear sir, would give rise to, I would at least have commanded that one or two of our regiments had stayed behind in the vicinity for our protection. As it is they are by now far in the south and we find ourselves at the mercy of the Republic. I can't even leave this damned city without arousing suspicion. And this all thanks to your mad escapade! Would you at least tell me the root cause of all this!" And, full of bitterness, he began to retie his shot-brocade trouser laces tighter round his thighs.*

"Monseigneur," Bougainville answered, "I can ask for no more than, with your permission, to be able to tell you all. It is for no other reason than that that I owe the honour of your visit…"

"What," La Trémoille cried, "you really want to tell me?"

"Correct."

"Well, go ahead then!" yelled the Marshal.

The report which Bougainville now delivered was first accompanied by furrowed brows, then by raised eyebrows with eyes dilated, finally by all the symptoms of anxiety which are easily understandable

* For over a century trouser laces were wound round the thighs, and for over a century they did not stay put, but slid down the legs. It was only in 1600 that trousers began to be fastened just below the knee. Truly, mankind needs a long time to progress one single step.

when one finds oneself confined in the same room as a madman. To cap it all, Bougainville demanded that the Marshal take personal charge of the liberation of Mona Lisa.

"My dear sir," La Trémoille said, getting up and not letting Bougainville out of his sight as he groped for his hat behind him, "my dear sir, not only am I not going to stick my nose in such insane undertakings, but I forbid you too in the strictest terms to contemplate such absurdities. Should you make the least attempt to the contrary, I shall deprive you of your dagger. The arrest under which I have put you naturally remains in force. Nor will you receive any visitors, instead you will employ the time and leisure which your confinement affords you to await the chirurgeon, whom I shall send to open one of your veins. I have spoken! God preserve you!"

And, ignoring the protestations and pleas which Bougainville gave rein to, he hastily left the room. The young man was plunged into the most heart-rending tumult. Had he not been certain of having found his beloved's grave empty, he wouldn't have been able to swear before God that he hadn't made a mistake and, like all the rest, he would have had to doubt his own sanity. In the meantime, his confusion and love were intensified by the obstacles confronting him, the unattainability of his beloved and the fateful star which hovered over his undertaking, to the point where he really thought he was on the brink of insanity. In any case, it struck him as completely unthinkable that he should remain incarcerated within the four walls. After a short period of reflection, he therefore decided to disobey La Trémoille's command and set out again on the quest for the missing woman. If he were only to find her, of which he still had not the slightest doubt that he would, he could be assured of the Marshal's pardon.

In the course of the afternoon, in the sweltering August heat, he went on horseback, accompanied by his servants, searching through two estates which were pointed out to him as belonging to Giocondo, and all for nothing, for even if the detainee might have been hidden there, after what happened yesterday it was safe to assume that Ser Francesco had already found a more secluded hiding place for her.

The houses, the vineyards, the gardens and the groves which Bougainville searched were totally unfamiliar to him. And yet it seemed to him that he'd already visited them in his dreams in the distant past.

As evening fell, after spending the last few hours without having said a word, pierced though the heart by the memory of the beloved girl's smile as if by poisonous arrows, he returned home to the city with a desperate resolve brewing in his bosom to pay Ser Francesco another visit, to put a knife to his breast and force him to yield up his secret.

Nondescript grey and flamingo-coloured clouds hung motionless in the silver-grey air.

As ill luck would have it, Bougainville, about to dismount in front of Giocondo's house, suddenly spotted in the murky half-light a nobleman in the company of two servants in an alleyway who was about to enter the house. Bougainville immediately climbed off his horse and rushed towards him.

"A word, if you please, Monsieur!" he said in French as he barred the way.

"Monsieur," replied the nobleman, a handsome though slightly supercilious young man with dark blue eyes and eyebrows that extended right across the bridge of his nose, also in French, "how may I be of service to you?" And he cast a quick glance at Bougainville and the group of flunkeys standing behind him with their horses.

"Are you," Bougainville asked, "acquainted with Ser Francesco del Giocondo? May I, for the sake of further information which I'd like to solicit from you, enquire if you are indeed well acquainted with him?"

"Very well, as a matter of fact," the nobleman responded, "so much so that I intend to pay him a visit to express my commiseration regarding certain events which occurred last night at his house."

"And what kind of events were they?" Bougainville asked, frowning.

"An idiot," the nobleman said, and since Bougainville was French, the former took particular care to enunciate every word individually, "an idiot, accompanied by a number of Monsieur La Trémoille's cavaliers, forced his way into the house and demanded at all costs to know the whereabouts of Ser Francesco's long-deceased wife. Since I'm not only a friend of his but was quite close to the deceased too, I consider it my duty to testify my abhorrence at such a gross violation of the dead person's memory." And with these words he looked into the eyes of the Frenchman with proud disdain.

"My worthy Gentiluomo," Bougainville said, placing his hand on his hip and at the same time feeling blood rush to his face in rage, "would you mind telling me kindly who you are, after which I shall, for a reason which you are about to find out, also disclose to you my name!"

"I can easily," the nobleman said, "grant you that favour. For your information, I am Amerigo Capponi!"

"And I," Bougainville yelled, "my dear Messer Capponi, seeing that you are not only deceiving Ser Francesco but have the effrontery to visit him in his house—I am no other than the idiot who broke into his house yesterday, and you are going to fight me now!"

"I wouldn't even dream of it," Capponi exclaimed contemptuously. "You are a certified madman, and

I've no intention whatsoever of crossing arms with every demented upstart. Get out of my way! Off with you!"

"Sir," Bougainville yelled, reaching for his dagger and pointing it at his opponent, "you're a coward! But you are mistaken if you believe you can get away from me with your smooth talk! Draw if you don't want me to skewer a defenceless man to the wall like a rat!"

"That's enough!" Capponi retorted. "I can't put up with your ravings any longer! Make way!—Hey there, guards!" he called out in Italian, clapping his hands. "Get this imbecile out of the way!"

At this command Capponi's men immediately rushed forward and fell with their clubs upon Bougainville, who was hard put to ward off their blows. However, at this his own men were quick to enter the fray. Soon several passers-by participated in attacking the French. A riot ensued, everybody shouting, "To arms, to arms!" And everyone seemed to join in. In the heat of the affray, Capponi too felt obliged to draw his dagger. However, it was barely out of its sheath when one of Bougainville's servants, having stolen up to him from the back, grabbed him by the neck. Capponi let go of the dagger, fell forward under the servant's weight and the blade went right through his body.

When they turned him over his eyes were already shut; only his eyelids with their long, almost feminine lashes still quivered imperceptibly and a reddish foam was gathering round his mouth.

He died as he was carried into Giocondo's house.

AFTER THE DEATH OF CAPPONI, who was the son of one of the foremost Florentines, La Trémoille could do nothing to save Bougainville's life. The rabble that had congregated around the Marshal's residence was so menacing that he would have liked to wheel out his artillery were it not for the fact that the pieces, which Monsieur de Amboise had commissioned the founders to cast for him from church bells at the expense of the Milanese, had long ago trundled on their way to Umbria. It was clear that there was no way of leaving the city without an appropriate atonement, and it was just a matter of time before La Trémoille's residence would be sacked. It was for this reason that he decided to make a sacrifice of Bougainville.

He condemned him to death by the sword.

Before his execution the young man had only one wish remaining: to see Giocondo's wife.

Instead he was visited in his room—which was now his prison cell, with a strong guard posted outside not so much to forestall his flight as to save him from being torn to pieces by a lynch mob—by Leonardo.

"You poor, misguided man!" the painter exclaimed. "So you still do not believe that she is long dead!"

"Who?" Bougainville asked.

"Gioconda, of course! Ser Francesco's wife. The root cause of your incurable passion! Are you really mad then?"

Bougainville did not reply straightaway; he clenched his teeth and said at last, "Is it true then that this woman really no longer exists? I have to assume you are speaking the truth, my dear sir. Because no one would deceive a man who is about to die."

"Of course I'm telling you the truth!" Leonardo exclaimed. "And I've always been telling it. Only, in your madness, you refused to believe it, unfortunate man that you are!"

Bougainville shrugged his shoulders and looked down; at last he said:

"Incidentally, why do you call me unfortunate, Messer Leonardo? I would have been unfortunate only if I'd stayed alive, for, so long as I'd have lived, I wouldn't have found Mona Lisa. But as it is, I'm going to see her very soon."

"Monsieur," Leonardo said, "when a man who is faced as you are with an event which is, in the end, perhaps overrated, but nevertheless greatly feared—because of certain weaknesses which Nature has intentionally given us—one ought not to want to take certain comforting thoughts away from him. The Turks and Moors will insist that it's only in heaven that they will first savour those earthly delights after which you, too, have hankered, but which have led to your destruction in the first place. Gentleman to gentleman though, frankly and without prevarication, but above all as one man of spirit to another, although to be sure you have failed to live up to that calling, I will say this to you: I'm afraid that you're as unlikely to meet your beloved in heaven as you were on earth. I'm perfectly aware that you, condemned to die as you are, could accuse me of heresy. I can moreover assure you that I've no truck with either the fantasies of the dying or the fears of the living, with either heaven or hell. Neither the expectation of the bliss of faith in the next world nor of delights in some kind of earthly paradise-to-come can sustain us in this world. What can give us strength is solely the delight we derive from truth and beauty, from morality and a sense of honour."

"My dear sir," Bougainville responded after a short silence, "you could well be right on this score, that nothing in the next world will come to us as cheaply as the Church would have us believe. You are wrong, though, to dismiss the idea lock, stock and barrel. I have, in the hours that have so far been granted to me, thought about all this, and I tell you, there are some things that are eternal and undying. Above all, my dear sir—love. The loving embrace in which two souls are locked is far stronger than the bodily clinch of two corporeal lovers. But it's hardly necessary to split love into bodily and sublime, into earthly and divine. In the end there is only one love. Because it is the only thing that unifies everything. Nothing is capable of separating two people who love each other—these binary stars eternally revolving round each other—not even God. One need only have been truly in love to realize that all else, heaven and hell included, is as nothing in comparison. There is also no actual death. In truth, there is one thing only—love. Do you not also find this to be so?"

Leonardo did not respond; he kept his silence and looked thoughtfully at this young man whom he had just now considered totally insane and who, by virtue of the grandeur of his sentiments, had humbled the artist.

"And now," Bougainville continued, "now tell me also how it was at all possible that I could have assumed Giocondo's wife was still alive? That she wasn't in her grave! That it appeared inconceivable for me that she was dead!"

"Very easily," Leonardo said. "It was very easily possible. You fell in love with her. In addition, I have looked into the matter and discovered that she really does not lie buried in the Santa Croce tomb. She died during the plague. Hooded men came and buried her somewhere along with dozens or hundreds of other corpses. Giocondo, however, could not in view of his own and her family lineage allow the word to get around that she was buried in a communal grave. That is the secret of which you became a victim.

Still, you may comfort yourself with one thought. Did I not tell you once that the woman one paints is never real? And so in reality one loves only the woman that does not really exist."

"Why should I comfort myself with that?" Bougainville asked. "Love does not need any comforting. It does not even need requiting. All it needs is itself."

And then he was hauled out of the prison, taken to the Old Market and beheaded.

The execution was carried out in full view of the inhabitants of the city, and the Marshal and his suite, the Gonfaloniere della Giustizia Piero Soderini, many members of the Signoria and a large number of the nobility as well as da Vinci were also present. The sight of the surging populace, the glare of the polished armour in the brilliant sunlight, the awesome cape of the executioner, the flash of the sword, the riot of colours and human forms were truly inspiring. Leonardo alone regarded everything with indifference. Immediately after the execution he returned home and with a few strokes of the brush changed Gioconda's smile. He stood all the while

a little to the right of the picture, on the same spot
where Bougainville had once stood when he was
looking at it, and the eyes of the woman, turned
slightly to the left, regarded him in the same way as
they had Philippe de Bougainville. After Leonardo
had worked on the picture a little longer the smile was
transformed completely, and the artist said to himself
that it was now perfect. It was totally enchanting,
both mysterious and enigmatic; it was impossible
to tell if she smiled at Bougainville or whether she
was luring him into very heaven; no one could tell
what it was she was smiling at.

The next day the Marshal pulled out of Florence
and headed for Naples; however, the light-footed
goddess of Victory eluded him, and in December
1503 he was beaten to destruction by the Spaniards
at Consalvo.

It was rumoured that Leonardo had spent four
more years ceaselessly working on La Gioconda; in
truth however he merely sat before it and stared at it.

When he moved to Milan he took it with him;
later he went with it to France, where he sold it to
King Francis I for a large sum of gold. Since then it

has been regarded as the most famous picture in the world, and is at present in Paris. There too no end of people fell in love with it; one idiot over-painted it and a certain Vincenzo Perrugia, a glazier, stole it and later gave it back in Florence, no one knows why. Attempts were made to associate it with a tedious love affair in which a real woman had played a part. But the real grounds for this have not come to light. Nor is it ever likely that they shall. No one ever knows the real grounds for anything.

It has also been claimed that the picture in the Louvre is not authentic, but a fake. However, one would have to have no understanding whatsoever of the colossal stature of the painter or of love itself to insist that this was in fact true.

PUSHKIN PRESS

Pushkin Press was founded in 1997, and publishes novels, essays, memoirs, children's books—everything from timeless classics to the urgent and contemporary.

This book is part of the Pushkin Collection of paperbacks, designed to be as satisfying as possible to hold and to enjoy. It is typeset in Monotype Baskerville, based on the transitional English serif typeface designed in the mid-eighteenth century by John Baskerville. It was litho-printed on Munken Premium White Paper and notch-bound by the independently owned printer TJ International in Padstow, Cornwall. The cover, with French flaps, was printed on Colorplan Pristine White paper. The paper and cover board are both acid-free and Forest Stewardship Council (FSC) certified.

Pushkin Press publishes the best writing from around the world—great stories, beautifully produced, to be read and read again.

STEFAN ZWEIG · EDGAR ALLAN POE · ISAAC BABEL
TOMÁS GONZÁLEZ · ULRICH PLENZDORF · TEFFI
VELIBOR ČOLIĆ · LOUISE DE VILMORIN · MARCEL AYMÉ
ALEXANDER PUSHKIN · MAXIM BILLER · JULIEN GRACQ
BROTHERS GRIMM · HUGO VON HOFMANNSTHAL
GEORGE SAND · PHILIPPE BEAUSSANT · IVÁN REPILA
E.T.A. HOFFMANN · ALEXANDER LERNET-HOLENIA
YASUSHI INOUE · HENRY JAMES · FRIEDRICH TORBERG
ARTHUR SCHNITZLER · ANTOINE DE SAINT-EXUPÉRY
MACHI TAWARA · GAITO GAZDANOV · HERMANN HESSE
LOUIS COUPERUS · JAN JACOB SLAUERHOFF
PAUL MORAND · MARK TWAIN · PAUL FOURNEL
ANTAL SZERB · JONA OBERSKI · MEDARDO FRAILE
HÉCTOR ABAD · PETER HANDKE · ERNST WEISS
PENELOPE DELTA · RAYMOND RADIGUET · PETR KRÁL
ITALO SVEVO · RÉGIS DEBRAY · BRUNO SCHULZ